Age with a Giggle

A HELPFUL LITTLE HANDBOOK ON AGING

by

SHARYN CHAPMAN

This book is a work of fiction. Names, characters, places and incidents are either the product of the author's imagination or are used fictitiously. Any resemblance to actual persons, living or dead, or to actual events or locales is entirely coincidental.

AGE WITH A GIGGLE, A HELPFUL LITTLE HANDBOOK ON AGING

The publisher does not have any control over and does not assume any responsibility for author or third-party websites or their content.

Images:
Copyright © Thinkstock/119113151/iStockphoto
Copyright © Thinkstock/ 98222792/iStockphoto
Copyright © Thinkstock/99815537/Hemera

Published by Telemachus Press, LLC
http://www.telemachuspress.com

Visit the author at
http://www. sharynchapman.com

Follow Sharyn Chapman on Twitter
https://twitter.com/#!/search/%40chapmanauthor

Visit Sharyn Chapman's Facebook Page
http://www.facebook.com/sharynchapmanauthor

ISBN# 978-1-938135-51-4 (eBook)
ISBN# 978-1-938135-52-1 (paperback)

Version 2012.06.12

Printed in the United States of America
10 9 8 7 6 5 4 3 2 1

Contents

This book is dedicated to my wonderful mother and to all women, tall, short, pink, blue or orange who are on the path of aging.

A special thank you to my sweet friend
and fellow author D. L. Houston
for all her hand-holding and guidance.

Introduction

This book has been written to assist all women who are searching for spiritual and emotional wisdom and a way to cope with aging. Women come in every size, shape and color and, although we are paradoxically different, we are truly the same. Our experiences might change because of the zillion and twelve variables in our individual lives but our issues, feelings and desires remain constant.

We are complex bodies of love and good deeds who very often shortchange ourselves. We find a benchmark and think it has to be our standard. We hate the changes we see in the mirror as the years pass by and feel we must struggle to hold on to our youth. Why? If anyone can make lemonade from wilted, sagging and dried up lemons, a woman can.

And then there are the life issues which seem to get more prevalent as time goes by. We want to make the best decisions for ourselves and our loved ones but sometimes we let old scars and ridiculous habits mar the surface of our thinking.

Humor can help us find our way. If we begin each day feeling like we are going into gum surgery, how can we feel joy? Re-ignite your ability to laugh and exhume the lightheartedness that you buried so many years ago.

Even though I have been curiously compelled to write this book, please do not think it is autobiographical in any way. Well, to be honest, maybe some of the information does pertain to me but I am not willing to tell you what. I have learned not to take myself too seriously but I am not crazy enough to open Pandora's Box completely!

Please know this tome is not intended to be used as a life guide. Instead, it is intended to encourage us all to forge ahead with grace and humor while making good life choices.

Where Did She Go?

It is amazing how young 60 years old seems to me and yet *who is this woman in the mirror*?

The word life is defined as the entire period during which somebody is, has been, or will be alive. We are all blessed to have the experience of life but for many of us it has not always been a lark in the park.

Life can be arduous and frequently frenetic. Day after day we are constantly challenged by the tedious tasks of our existence. The phone is ringing, kids are making demands on us, our husbands are bellowing about something they can't find. (Don't we know there is always something they can't find?) Who has the time to think about anything, especially our looks? Who says, "Oh, my, yesterday I had 11 gray hairs and eureka! Today, I have 14." Not even June Cleaver had that kind of time!

So, is it surprising that when we finally do take the time to examine our looks that we might get a shock? What was pert and lovely might now be dilapidated and dwindling. What was firm and tight could now be mushy and dimply. Dimples on kids' faces are cute but dimples on women's legs are **not** so cute.

Age is sly in how it creeps up and slowly sabotages perfectly good bodies. The process is so gradual that it is indiscernible on a daily basis. Yet with the accumulation of years, what we see in the mirror can put fear into the most fearless of women. What happened to our youth?

Whether we like it or not, we are on the journey of aging. Now don't get me wrong. I love living and appreciate every day I am granted to do so. I also admit these thoughts might seem shallow and yet — aren't they shared by us all?

Even though we are at the point where our investment in health insurance is beginning to pay off only too well, we can still slow the aging process by taking good care of ourselves. However, in the end we have to be realists and admit that our bodies are going to change and age whether we like it or not.

I was born into a middle-class family that is as wholesome as apple pie at a church social. I am the only child of parents who loved me unconditionally and cared for me in the very best way. We always dined as a family on delicious and nutritious home-cooked meals. Our recreation was camping so I always got lots of fresh air and exercise. My stress levels were so low they did not even register on the charts! It was utopia as I now think back.

From that point on, my life had its ups and downs but throughout it all, I have always put a premium on exercise and healthy living. Why do I bore you with this self indulging information? Because, it makes my point about aging. No one escapes. No amount of preparation can totally stop the clock. No one can predict what their fate will be.

OK, big deal, you say. Well, for a person who has worked hard at staying young, *it is*. SAG YOU ARE IT is not the game I expected to play in my "golden years." This process of becoming older has turned out to be a really dirty trick played by my geriatric genes. Now, being a practical person and not wanting to join the hordes of women who spend their money on newly reconfigured bodies, head to toe, I am deciding that I need an attitude adjustment. If God graces me with another 30-40 years, I want to take pleasure in them and not live in the land of regret, longing for the "old me."

So instead of saying, "Where did she go," I am more interested in "who is she now."

~~~~~

My Old Face Is Mismatched With My Young Mind.

~~~~~

Be The Person
God Was Hoping For

There are several stages of life. Birth to infancy begins the journey. We all come into the world free of prejudices, worries, anger and with pure hearts. The world is our oyster. We accept and appreciate what we have been given and with a sharp slap on the back we are raring to go.

The next stage is childhood. We are now little sponges wicking up knowledge at an amazing rate. We are free of any encumbrances and ask only for love and nurturing. This stage brings with it new discovery and great excitement. Interaction from those both in and outside of the family is experienced and welcomed. Now is the time we unknowingly begin to decide who we are.

The stage of adulthood is the most critical and usually the most difficult. We now *think* we know what life is about. We feel strongly that we have a direction and work to accomplish what we feel is appropriate and expected.

Depending upon who and what has influenced us so far, we might start to exhibit some negative qualities and ideas. Most of us are not even aware we are doing it. What should be most important in our lives can get misplaced or confused in our minds. We do not always make the best choices—but do we see this?

The final chapter, which should be the age of full maturity, *can be* our best years. You notice I do not refer to it as old age because we all know that we are only as old as we *think*! If we insist on thinking like an old person we will have no choice other than to be an old person. If we think young, we have a better chance of staying young.

Now this is important, so listen up kids. I maintain that this is the period of your life that you finally have a chance to get it right! I don't care about all your extraordinary accomplishments. I am talking about fixing relationships, mending fences and leaving this world a better place because of your counsel and your actions. You might say, "*I am too old to change. I am, who I am, so accept who I am.*" Well, I say, get over yourself!

Don't allow previous mistakes to define you. Begin today to mold the new, improved version of yourself and share it with others. This is the time of your life in which the wisdom you have accumulated over the years should be used and imparted to everyone you care about.

~~~~~

If You Want To Be Young, Be.

David Thoreau

~~~~~

That idea might sound scarier to you than a Stephen King novel and yet it can be easier to accomplish than you think. One small step leads to another. Let go of any unhealthy thoughts. Reach out to those you love and be sure they know how you feel. Make amends with those you have damaged.

Don't stop there. Be a special person to **anyone** in need. You might be amazed at how it brightens your own day. Put petty grievances back to a place where they cannot upset you. See a wrong and make it right. You have the power to do all of these things, *so do them!*

You know we each have a time clock on our heads. Who knows what tomorrow will bring? It is up to each of us to use this precious time wisely and productively so we can be sure that when it is time to check out, we do so on a high note, without remorse or unfinished business. In other words, make your life count!

~~~~~

Age Is Strictly A Case
Of Mind Over Matter.
If You Don't Mind,
It Doesn't Matter.

Jack Benny

~~~~~

Perky Packed Its Bags And Moved To Pitiful

In the process of aging, humor has always come to my rescue. In the most dire of circumstances, I have found salvation in my ability to laugh.

There was a time when I would take my abundant energy for granted. When perky packed its bags and moved to pitiful, I began to succumb to the dark side. I had to find the humor in it. How, you say, can you? That magnificent marvel called energy, which had motored my boat, has now left me in permanent dry dock.

The Only Exercise I Got Today Was Jumping To Conclusions.

So, what does a girl do? She makes the best of what she has. I want the energy of a 16-year old, and yet would **never** want to go back to a point where I had to take algebra again. Remember the days when you could leap small buildings and not even break a sweat? I would like to think I am still capable of that but know better than to try. Just the thought of leaping anything at 60 makes me sweat.

A Bicycle Cannot Stand On Its Own Because It Is Two-Tired!

Speaking of breaking a sweat, have you heard about Menopause? Of course you have. I call it God's practical joke on womankind. Some of us are still trying to slay that monster. One good thing is by the time we reach maturity, we do not have to deal with our monthly "friend." I will confide that I never really considered it a friend but instead a messy, unpredictable pain in the pelvic area. But—this so-called friend did bring along some good company, in the name of Miss Estrogen. That handy hormone kept me from looking like the Sahara.

Dried Up Eggs Make For A Poor Omelet

It is said that a woman's beauty begins to fade when her production years are over and she no longer has the need to attract the opposite sex for procreation. What is that about?

I would like to continue to look young and be thought of as beautiful. If all things were fair and just, we **would** get more beautiful as we aged.

But just a minute, maybe we do. I look at my mom and see **nothing but beauty**. Oh sure, she would tell you she has her share of wrinkles, but I defy anyone to meet her and not see love and beauty. So perhaps the trick is to look **beyond the mirror**. We might now find it increasingly difficult to maintain outer beauty but we **can** learn how to show more inner beauty–beauty I call, BEAUTY OF THE HEART.

~~~~~

Women Break More Hips Than Promises.

~~~~~

Beauty Of The What?

Beauty of the heart is just as it sounds. Showing kindness, tenderness and generosity is all it requires. It is really what we women do best.

We Love To Show Love.

As parents, we have a responsibility to our children to provide and care for them. If we are doing our jobs well, we know how to make our offspring happy and keep them healthy. We always demonstrate our love and it is appreciated by our diminutive progeny.

This condition of love seems to further ramp up when it comes to grandparents. Those of us fortunate enough to have garnered this title enjoy exuding complete, genuine and unadulterated love to these little cherubs. Perhaps, by this time in our lives we have become perfectly proficient at showing love.

Careful observation will also demonstrate how this adoration is returned. It is just a deliciously comfortable feeling that grandchildren have when in the company of older people. Kids seem to be naturally attracted to the aura of love that their grandparents give off.

This pure devotion most often will come not from a place of responsibility but, rather, diametrically from the heart. Children, from infancy on, ***just get this***. There is nothing more beautiful than listening to babies coo in the arms of their grandmothers while gazing happily into their eyes.

It does not stop there. As miniature minors they continue to revel in all the attention that grandparents give, blissfully lapping it up. With a little time and diligence, beautiful bonds can be created and, if we play our cards right, these bonds will continue well after we all exit the earth.

How happy this is for everyone! How great do parents feel when ***their*** most important possessions are adored and cherished? It is wonderful for them to know that the special relationships that they have had with their own parents have now been extended to their family.

If you have done **nothing else** in your life to be proud of, you can **still do this**. Even if your relationship with your own children is lacking, even if no one ever showed you how you can still be that life example to your grandkids. They will instinctively respond and everyone will be so grateful to you for sharing **your** beauty of the heart.

~~~~~

Giving To Other Feels Good.
Be Careful, You Might Begin
To Like Yourself.

~~~~~

I've Got Hair Where?

But, I digress. I have yet to mention all the other lovely gifts Mr. Menopause brings. Remember how thick and luxurious your hair used to be? Now, each day I find I can make a blanket from what I discover in my hair brush.

At some point in time, loss of hair in women over a certain age must have seemed like a proper and reasonable plan. Not to fret however as *now* we have new hair popping up in so many *other* locations.

I'm sorry, but it is *just not sexy* when you are tripping over chin hairs and yet-there they are. When your husband hands you his nose-hair trimmer, take him seriously. He is on to something and it's not pretty.

The good news is, shaving your legs daily turns into a weekly activity at the most. This, of course, gives you more time to manage your newly acquired mustache.

~~~~~

You Never Grow Old In Your Head.

~~~~~

Genius Borders On Insanity

Another treat we women experience are hot flashes. Or should I say cold feet? Or should I say hot flashes **with** cold feet? Yes ladies, that **is** possible and is experienced by the most elite of women. Years ago women were institutionalized for their "strange actions" during menopause. Maybe these women knew something we don't, as this **would** be a clever way of getting a long, overdue and well deserved rest. Genius, if you ask me.

What about this new-fangled dry skin that has suddenly made an appearance? You know about it. Don't try to look surprised. Our skin is our largest organ and mine is playing a melancholy tune. I moisturize so much that you would think I would slip out of a chair, and yet people still compliment me on my alligator shoes when I am barefoot.

Dryness has an impact on more than the skin. I won't go there except to say when you age, you dry up. How positively brilliant! But no! that is not all. Guess what? You can also leak.

Yes, that too. How many of us have had to change our underwear after a sneeze? At night I am up and down like a toilet seat at a mixed beer party. Don't even think of telling me a joke without getting out of the way from the direct path to the bathroom. My friends call me Miss Thimble Bladder and with good reason but–I have noticed that *they also* never pass up a rest room.

I could go on and on, but the simple fact is that after a certain age the body has changed. We can't sleep but we do creak, we can't poop but we do droop, we are sincere but we can't hear, what we see is to a lesser degree and who can remember that it is December?

When we find our humor, we find our joy.

~~~~~

The Secret Of Staying Young
Is To Live Honestly, Eat Slowly
And Lie About Your Age.

Lucille Ball

~~~~~

A pleasant looking older woman goes to a bar. The bartender recognizes her and says hi Gracie, would you like your usual? Gracie nodded and the bartender prepared her drink of vodka on the rocks with two drops of water. As he handed her the drink she told him she was celebrating her 80th birthday. The bartender smiled and said, "Happy Birthday Gracie. Your drink is on the house.

As Gracie was finishing her drink the woman seated to her right said, "Give this lovely lady another drink and it will be *my* birthday treat to her."

Delighted to hear this, Gracie accepted and ordered her second vodka on the rocks with two drops of water. As the bartender handed Gracie the drink he said, "I am puzzled, Gracie. Why do you never want more than two drops of water in your drink?"

"It is because at age 80 a woman will never have any trouble holding her liquor but holding her water is another issue."

How To Be Sexy When It Won't Move Anymore

When I was younger, getting up in the morning was so easy. I could bound out of bed and go immediately into a run, my body as pliable as Silly Putty.

Those then toned and supple muscles have now begun to feel inflexible and stiff. I can't remember **when** I began to feel this way but gone are the days of having nothing to complain about. Here an ache, there an ache. Bending over to tie your shoe can set off a series of land mines that will put you in bed for a week.

Subtle changes start to set in. First they are small and insignificant but when we are not looking they can grow to a great big pain in the, well you know. The unsmug reality is these so-called glorious golden years are highly over rated.

I foolishly thought I was in control of my fate but I soon learned when you make plans in life, God laughs. I meet people with new knees, hips, shoulders and pray that will never be me and yet for some of us it does happen. I call it:

Things that happen in the night.

No one can stop the natural process of aging but continuing to stay active and engaged in life is critical. Use your sense of humor to make the best of what you have. Instead of mourning the loss of your youthful body, spend your time practicing how to be sexy on a walker. Don't laugh, it's doable. We are women. With a little determination and a great deal of attitude we can accomplish anything.

~~~~~

Why Would You Sit When You Could Dance?

~~~~~

Backdoor Melodrama

I went to the gynecologist last week for him to look under the hood. Ladies, this is a must. If you have not been yet this year, make your appointment today! If it was a necessary appointment for anyone else in your life you know you would get right on it. We must always give ourselves the same care we would give our loved ones.

That being said, this yearly checkup does not exactly promise to be an enjoyable experience. When I left the house for my appointment, I said to my husband "I am off to be naked in front of a relative stranger and have him evaluate the condition of my who-who. "Interestingly enough, when I mentioned where I was going, my husband sent me off with,"That's my girl, have a good time." Is he kidding? Does he know anything about what is involved?

So after waiting for over an hour in a frigid waiting area, I am politely escorted into a small changing room. I am asked to remove all of my clothing and put on a dressing gown which was definitely designed by a man. No style, no protection from the elements and an open front door! Being the cooperative person I am, I do not complain.

A smiling nurse then escorts me to another small room with a large, intimidating machine. This modern age torture device is determined to make pancakes out of what is left of my once, pert breasts. My 36 Cs are *already* 36 longs. Of course there is an advantage to this as now going braless does pull some of the wrinkles out of my face.

But, I digress. After experiencing discomfort of mammoth proportion while reciting all the reasons I intend to ask to be reincarnated next time as a man, the still smiling nurse then leads me to the pelvic examination room for more fun.

I have a wonderful doctor with a great sense of humor who makes this process easier, but let's get real. Who can relax while four pieces of equipment and two hands are searching their abandoned mine?

"How are you," he asks as he searches around? "Oh, I haven't had this much fun since childbirth," I say. He laughs, picks up his wares and is on to his next victim. I leave, walking slightly slower than when I arrived. Oh well, I am proud of myself. This less than entertaining but very important exam is complete for another year. Later that night when my husband starts suggesting a roll in the hay my answer is, "That's my boy, have a good time."

~~~~~

Laugh And You'll Live Without Medicaid Until You're 100

Julie Newmar

~~~~~

Thin Thighs
And All Things Sacred

Do you ever hear the theme from Jaws when you see yourself naked in front of a mirror? How about when you try to fit into that cute little black cocktail dress you just **had** to buy last year?

You have been **mostly** eating sensibly and exercising **some** and yet you still have stuff. Stuff that you know was not there before and you could happily live without now. I have read that we all are born with a set amount of fat cells and they stay with us for a lifetime. Can you tell me why fat cells are with us forever and yet brain cells seem to take a hike?

We have talked about the dimpling which begins to happen on our skin's surface. **This is just wrong**. You can exercise all day, all night Maryanne and still have this happen. Why, you ask? Should we look to our ancestors? They **could** be the reason that your smooth, supple thighs now resemble cottage cheese.

Our genes do play a significant role in determining how we age but are they the only governing factor? In a word, no. Environment, stress levels, inadequate sleep and overall pitiful personal care are just a few of the other influences which will have an impact on our bodies. Some of these factors I know I can control and I do try, but still my mirror insists on introducing me to a different person almost every time I look.

Then there is this newly acquired luggage I have recently discovered under my eyes. A sign of beauty, **I think not**. I have taken to wearing sunglasses whenever possible. Not only are they concealing but they do give me the mysterious appearance I have always longed for. You see, there is always an answer. You just have to look for it.

The recent addition of a wattling turkey neck is also less than charming. I have a drawer full of scarves which I have learned to tie more efficiently than Houdini. Fortunately, my sagging neck **does** fit in nicely with my double chin. I can tell you that a double chin does not mean double pleasure. However, it does make for a convenient additional stop for food to make before it reaches my Gucci blouse.

~~~~~

Beauty Comes In All Ages, Colors, Shapes And Forms. God Never Makes Junk.

Kathy Ireland

~~~~~

~~~~~

They Tell You That You'll Lose Your
Mind When You Grow Older.
What They Don't Tell You Is That
You Won't Miss It Very Much.

Malcolm Crowley

Don't Forget To Be Young,
When You Are Old.

~~~~~

My 60-Year-Old Stomach: The Accordion No One Wants To Play

I don't know about you, but I have come by my tummy honestly. I have worked very hard over a period of many years downloading cookies, cakes and glorious goodies to be where I am today. So why should I be surprised if now it is pompously protruding and preceding my arrival wherever I go?

Before Mr. Metabolism faded I was doing fine. I would enjoy decadence and after a brisk walk I would see no evidence of it. After Mr. Metabolism lost his interest and Miss Estrogen took a hike, suddenly everything I indulged in traveled to one spot or another and set up housekeeping.

Now, when I was expecting my son, whom I have always adored more than words can say, I was excited about tummy enlargement. I proudly carried him for nine months without even a stretch mark to prove it. But guess what? He is now 35 and I still have a tummy. So be it.

We all have something we wish was not part of our view when we look in the mirror but we can't let it spoil our day. Remember, we are all sweet vestiges of unmatched designed beauty.

~~~~~

Jewelry Takes People's Minds Off Your Wrinkles.

Sonja Henie

~~~~~

What is that wrinkly thing by Grandma?
Good grief! It's Grampa!!

I have touched on the subject of dry skin but have yet to discuss wrinkled skin. Grandchildren think it is perfectly natural to see cavernous crevices on our faces. They couldn't care less if we grannies come in the lined or unlined version.

Some of us do care, however, and will choose to erase those lines. I do not fault them as we all have the right to make our own personal decisions. For some women, a strategic nip and tuck could allow them to like better what they see in the mirror. I do wonder, however, if erasing these less-than-desirable mini maps from our faces will diminish what we have done to earn them.

I guess this decision has no right or wrong answer. If you do choose to spend your retirement savings and follow the gaggles of girls going this route, please select the best professional you can afford. There is no sense in scrimping with substandard surgeons.

My arms have been fighting their own battle as well. We women lug around kids, dogs and you name what else for years to the point that our arms should look like we are ready for World Wide Wrestling. Instead we find drooping skin that insists on hanging around.

It really makes us reluctant to wear short sleeved or sleeveless garments. Now if these wings would allow me to take flight, I might appreciate them. Since they do not, I simply chalk it up to another test of my patience.

But, let's ponder this. Yes, Ma'am. I might be *just* the person to start a revolt of this thinking. Why do we feel our arms are **not** for public consumption? Ladies, I think it is time for *bare arms to unite*. Stand proud in your sleeveless dresses and challenge anyone who defies this action. Clever cover ups should not have a place in our lives.

We won't care that our stomach folds have grown to the point where we do not have a view of our navel. We will **not** defer going to the beach until long sleeved, floor length swimsuits are on the market. Let's stop hiding behind those sunglasses and break free of our fetters. This is **our time,** so let's make the most of it.

~~~~~

Wrinkles Should Merely Indicate Where Smile Lines Have Been

Mark Twain

~~~~~

Humor: It's Just Not For Kids Anymore

Eating to ward off your depression, a recession, or any aggression towards your mother, is *just not* a good idea. Your body is your temple.

HOW YOU CARE FOR IT
IS HOW IT WILL CARE FOR YOU

We all have had things happen to us in our lives that have not been enviable. Tragedy, loss, sadness, and mother issues are just a few. Some of us wonder how we have gotten this far in life in one piece.

However, placating yourself with improper and copious amounts of food, excessive and irresponsible drinking, smoking to beat the band is *not* your best game plan.

Let's talk about mothers. I have had girls say to me, "How is it possible that I am the product of a woman that I *just* cannot relate to?" *Well, move on, sister*. The simple truth, is *without her* you would not be here.

Forget your grievances and thank her for bringing you to the party. Whatever your concerns don't diminish the fact that she has given you the opportunity to live, love and laugh

Having said that, you do not have to be the exact person your mother and father created. **You** must decide how you want to celebrate life. Instead of being consumed by this over-packed baggage, store it away. Don't let it be your excuse for piling an over abundance of food on your plate each day.

The same goes for any other stress in your life. When life throws you a curve ball, catch it and throw it back. Now, you might say, "Doesn't that sound simple?" *My life is a mess* and all you have to offer is clichés!" OK, that is valid. But think about this: Did you know that laughter introduces endorphins into the body which are natural "feel good" hormones? These hormones help with emotional and even physical pain. Try to see the humor in everything, even when you have to dig miles to reach it.

~~~~~

The Older The Fiddler, The Sweeter The Tune.

An Old English Proverb

Middle Age Is When The Best Exercise Is One Of Discretion.

Laurence J. Peter

~~~~~

Eat Natural Food And Die Of Natural Causes

So what should we eat? What we are told is healthy and advisable today is possibly what will **kill us** tomorrow. Such confusion has us all talking to ourselves.

I say put your money where your mouth is. By that, I mean buy the best food **you** can afford. Vegan, smeagen. If you don't like vegetables and feel like eating more like a carnivore, then do it. Just do it with good quality and less quantity.

You Can't Get All Of Your Antioxidants From Wine.

Just for kicks, consider consuming a few vegetables and some delicious fruit. I know some of you would rather have an arm lopped off, but you should at least try.

Find your willpower and be an example to your kids. I know you remember this adage which is simple and clear, "Eat to live, **and don't live** to eat." Do not allow foods like sugar and corn syrup to control you. It is also not in your best interest to substitute unhealthy foods with chemicals and artificial ingredients for wholesome and natural cuisine.

Allow that wisdom to be known by all you care about. If you see your kids or your grandkids filling their tanks too often, intervene. You do not want to see them go down that slippery slope. After all, you can't let them get into that gallon of ice cream that you are saving for your now **infrequent** midnight binges.

~~~~~

To Live Another Day, Step Away From The Buffet

~~~~~

My Sister Forgot Her Coat And I Forgot My Sister

I used to pride myself on my keen memory. That seemingly simple function now presents more of a challenge. Holding on to a thought at this stage of the game takes more effort than getting into last year's jeans. A lot more determination and work is definitely now required to keep memory loss at bay.

Numerous activities are *constantly* being recommended to assist us in warding off this potential crisis, but do I really want to spend my valuable time writing the alphabet into diminutive boxes? Crossword puzzles be damned!

I still have a few senior cells inhabiting my precious brain, although they do pull off intermittent blunders. Some gaffes are more troublesome than others. The other day it was brought to my attention that I had forgotten to pull up my zipper. I was a little embarrassed, but that was better than what happened to my friend. She forgot to pull hers down.

Loss of memory does not happen overnight but slowly slips into sad disrepair like an unattended garden. In spite of taking a plethora of vitamins and minerals, loading up on antioxidants, and drinking enough water to hydrate a third world nation, memory can still fail. I know even the best of us forget and yet I have no patience for any malfunction of my anatomy. I tell people I repeat myself for emphasis. You can get away with that for a little while, anyway.

Wonder women that we are, we always found multitasking to be effortless. Couldn't we all hold the baby, fire up the BBQ and answer the phone with just one hand?

Multitasking, however, does require remembering what all the tasks were to be. Forgetting one thing, like not to leave the house before removing your teeth from the jar, can create a really humiliating and humbling *faux pas*.

Phone numbers for even the most insignificant acquaintances in my life used to be squirreled away carefully and could be accessed without delay. **Never** did I walk into a room and wonder why I was there or have to ask someone three times for the same answer.

When Did My Mind Start Operating Slower Than My Mouth?

Maybe ignorance is bliss, but can **small** lapses of memory really hurt me? Let's be positive. If our aging computers begin to shut down and can't be relied upon as much as they were in the past, we have to figure out how to make the best out of the situation.

Memory loss could have some advantages. Think about what fun you could have with your new life. Maybe you could pass off this new state of being as "crazy." You could finally get all of that which has been festering in you for years off your chest and those listening would do nothing but applaud you for your honesty. Any odd behavior on your part would be dismissed with a gentle shrug and a kind smile because everyone knows *you cannot argue with crazy*.

The next time I am faced with the dilemma of forgetfulness I will smile and say, "Who the hay cares? Who isn't in this position?" I intend to join the multi-numbered aging elders with grace.

Not remembering what makes me unhappy has to be a *plus*, and what does make me happy hopefully will always stay in the cargo space of my mind. To all those rotten suckers that seem to escape this problematic predicament, you do not worry me. I will refuse to remember who you are! Now didn't I tell you it was better to laugh?

~~~~~

Old People Do A Lot Of Thinking
About The Hereafter.

Not After They Are Gone
But When They Forget What
They Are Here After.

~~~~~

Why God Got It Wrong, But Maybe He Didn't

I feel strongly that some of these changes we experience cannot all be genetic. Let's be honest. Don't we all do things that are not in our best interest? Considering the abundance and diversity of opportunities to treat ourselves life is *just too tempting*.

We only go this way once (depending upon your own personal beliefs) so why **not** enjoy the ride? For those who believe they have a round-trip ticket I say, go for it honey. We all could be older than dirt if we have been this way a few times before.

BY THIS TIME IN OUR LIFE
WE SHOULD BE MAKING BETTER CHOICES

We have been told that we are here to learn lessons, so why are we still so enticed by food that our behavior of feeding our demanding fat cells continues **beyond being sensible**? I must admit I am not above this.

Personally, I think ice cream is the food of angels. Any flavor, any time, in great quantities. So when the results are in, some debris is bound to be left over after the storm. I understand that but **wish** it could be different.

I have long considered what I might say to God if I am fortunate enough to get a chance. I hesitate to criticize The Supreme Being, but why couldn't what we experience as children also be enjoyed in our maturity.

In my scenario, when you get older you would be able to stay up all night and still have boundless energy, indulge in what you want with no serious consequences and like the proverbial saying have the memory of an elephant. Wouldn't it be gratifying to be able to recall the names of everyone you had ever met?

Unfortunately, we did not get a vote on this so life goes on the way it was intended. Not **so** bad, really. Perfection is not possible, so let's just **make the most** of these years. Put complaints aside. Except for a very few people that we will **always** love to hate, (and you know who they are), we are all in the same slowly sinking vessel.

Smile! You are not taking on water yet!

~~~~~

Youth Is A Wonderful Thing. What A Crime To Waste It On Children.

George Bernard Shaw

~~~~~

Galloping Gossip
And Other
Mean-Spirited Acts

I have a tall, thin, beautiful friend whose company I enjoy. There are moments when it is a challenge, however. Comparing myself to her can make me feel like a small bundle of city trash. Do I let that get me down? No, I wear higher heels and make sure I don't have lipstick on my teeth.

The emerald eyed monster of envy MUST be curtailed. What happened to **women supporting women**? Why do I have to diminish **her** value to support my own?

How many times have you heard about women who insisted on tormenting each other with vicious venom? Even the quietest of disparaging whispers you utter get legs, and before long can reach the intended victim and be terribly hurtful.

Since **you** never want to be that unsuspecting target, why not show others that you are above this sorry behavior. Now you may say, "But getting even is fair. Why **can't** I enjoy being the tortuous talebearer that **she** is?"

Well, the real answer is that a sharp tongue can cut your own throat. My philosophy in life is: **support the person or avoid the person**. It is a big world out there. There are plenty of other people to be in the company of. Be ahead of the curve. Take the high road and move on.

You might think this point of view is suited for only the Pollyannas in the world and you could be right, but, doesn't it have to start somewhere? Setting this example could become contagious. Until we all go to that place of peace and forgiveness, none of us will truly evolve.

So the lesson seems to be: at any age we should not fall into the trap of comparing ourselves to another or we will never be satisfied. Not easy to do, I know. I find myself at times looking at my darling, young and beautiful daughter-in-law and wondering how, in a blink of an eye, I got from there to here. Now, I am not exactly destined for desperation in the looks department, but certainly anyone without a common sense bypass is bound to notice the differences between us.

I would love to still have all the gifts that came with my youth, but being the pragmatic person that I am, I know that ship has sailed. So instead, I am determined to believe that people will see the other gifts I bring now and they will not be distracted by the package they arrive in.

The baton has been passed—so be it. Come on, it's not as bad as it sounds. I am not, at this mature age, **expected** to look like at teenager, so if I just try to look great for **my** age, isn't that enough?

Yes, because I know if all of my focus is on **then**, I will lose the value of **now**. I intend to show I am suitably sanguine and very grateful for being fortunate enough to still be on the green side of the grass.

I will continue to exercise and take reasonable care even though maintenance is more and more time consuming and difficult. I will let the scale keep me honest. (I call it my morning dose of conscience.) I will think before I act particularly when it relates to my well-being, and choose to do what is wiser and not easier.

I also will not succumb to buying hyped-up beauty products that I would have to mortgage my house to own. Thanks to Mr. Lincoln, slavery went out many moons ago. No one can be a slave to their looks and expect to live a happy life. Moderation in all you do will be more fulfilling.

Life in balance is the key

Now that you have had time to think this over, consider taking that $100 you were going to throw away on **miracle** face cream and instead contribute it to a good cause. Doing this or performing any other act of kindness will positively guarantee that you will look **and** feel maaaaaaaaaaaavelous!

~~~~~

You Only Live Once, But If You Do Things Right, It Will Be Enough.

Mae West

~~~~~

~~~~~

A young boy watched his grandmother apply face cream. "Why do you do that?" he asked. "To make myself beautiful," said the grandmother as she wiped off the excess cream. The boy looked surprised. "So why are you taking it off? Are you giving up?"

~~~~~

A little boy was with his mother when they met an elderly, rather wrinkled woman his mom knew. The boy studied her for a while and then asked, "Why doesn't her skin fit her face?"

~~~~~

So Many Candles, So Little Cake

I know so many women who positively *refuse* to admit their age. They spend their lives going to great lengths to conceal the number of birthdays they have experienced. I appreciate that point of view and yet do not share it. I find celebrating anything in my life to be wonderful. When it comes to birthdays I am over the top with joy in anticipation of the upcoming event. I would shout the number from the rooftops if given the opportunity.

Being a Leo, I start the month with an announcement to all who will listen. I continue to discuss this self-determined momentous event every opportunity I get. Why, you ask? Well, the honest answer is because I love to feel special and enjoy any chance I get to rejoice in my life. Why would I *not* share my pleasure with everyone?

A jaded person might say I was really looking for the perks that birthdays bring. Wrong.

The most wonderful gift
I could ever receive,
I have already been given

My life has indescribable, enormous value to me and any other gift received is diminished by comparison.

Having said that, I have to admit that receiving presents can make life a little more special. I will not attempt to stop people in my life from indulging me but will accept graciously all that is given and try *never* to forget to say thank you.

I do not feel only *my* birthday is special. I relish the opportunity to celebrate any birthdays that come my way. I have a birthday book which rivals Webster's Dictionary and I love sending my congratulations to each person in it.

Each birthday we celebrate allows us more time to accomplish what we have set out to do in life. ***Don't sit home working on your obituary.*** Get out there and enjoy life. I personally have many more fish to fry, so I am putting in my requisition for countless more birthdays. Hello, are you listening up there?

~~~~~

Doctor, do you think I will live to 100? "Well," the doctor said "Do you do drugs, get too much sun, gamble, drive fast cars and have lots of sex?"

"No, "Said the man, "I don't do any of those things."

The doctor then replied, "Then why would you care?"

~~~~~

Going In For Parts

We live in a world where amazing feats of medicine can heal by replacing and repairing our tired-out, used up body parts. People with one, two or a plethora of problems hasten to their doctors in hopes of curing what ails them. New joints, new organs, new lenses in eyes, anything it takes to prevent our demise. For what they can't fix is prescribed a nice pill. How else can they justify their six-page bill?

The Body Heals The Ailment.
The Treatment Heals The Doctor!

Our eyes are on a downward spiral which literally changes how we see the world. Beyond surgery, eyeglasses should be an easy fix to this problem however, they come with problems of their own. Groping around for them in the night before I dare to set a foot on the floor is something I could do without.

Yes, glasses can be elusive. These necessary evils seem to have a mind of their own. I am sure I know where I left them and still they are not there. Is it possible that they can travel to points unknown when you are not looking or is it *more* likely that the lack of memory is rearing its ugly head again?

I take my glasses on and off so many times during a day that I now consider it part of my exercise routine. The wonderfully successful eye surgeries that are now possible are very alluring, and many of us will choose to take the plunge but for the time being I will continue to be content with my less than gratifying goggles.

Hearing loss is also debilitating for many of us to some degree. We think we are prepared for any inevitability and yet, *how annoying this is to us*! No one wants to miss out on what is happening around them. I remember having to speak up loudly so my grandparents could hear what I was saying and now I find myself asking those in the room to turn up the volume *for me*.

There is also something called selective hearing, and any woman on this globe who is married will know what I mean. Husbands are *very* proficient at this. My theory is, after some period, tedium can settle into a marriage and this is when men begin to turn off what they call "the blab."

It is amazing how they can so effectively filter out what they do not care to hear and yet would never miss a baseball score being announced two blocks away. So, with the aggressive voice of a linebacker, we repeat what they have just missed and allow them to plead innocence. This self-imposed condition requires a great deal of patience from an already overtaxed wife but don't kid yourselves boys. We girls have already figured you out.

Some of us will be luckier than others, but we all eventually get to the same place. It is as if each of our components have expiration dates and when they, in turn, cease to be current, we find ourselves potentially, significantly changed. That thought can be as disheartening to us as snow shoveling in the winter is to an Eskimo.

So my lassies, let's face facts. No matter how many parts we replace we are still on this obstacle riddled road and cannot turn back. So what is the secret to staying happy? In a word, laughter! It *is* the best medicine.

Keep putting on those patches that effectively hold you together and then spend the rest of the time empowering yourself to feel and show contentment. Happiness will abound if you refuse anything else.

~~~~~

No One Has To Tell Us How Many Beans Make Five!

~~~~~

~~~~~

There was a 90 year old man celebrating his birthday by staying in a fancy hotel. His children decided as his gift, would send a call girl to his room. When this young, attractive woman arrived she said to the elderly gentleman,
"I am here to give you super sex."

His reply was, "I will take the soup, thank you."

~~~~~

My Husband, My Hero

The simple truth, is men just have it easier than women as they age. Of course they have to pay attention to what they eat and should at least *try* to keep their bodies moving, but as a rule, many of them saunter through life without the appearance issues that women encounter.

Baldheaded, beer-gutted men still think they are beautiful. How about all those men who wear shorts no matter how their legs look! Do their brains not recognize the difference between strong, muscular, tanned limbs and scrawny, pale, blue-lined extremities? *Maybe,* men just have more self-confidence.

Most men tell me that wrinkles on men add character. This must be true because if you ask any plastic surgeon if he could make a living on only male patients he would tell you hands down no.

Unlike men, determined damsels feel they must carry the burden of retaining a youthful appearance. Sure, men will cavalierly say how foolish that thought is and to stop sweating the small stuff but do they really mean it?

How many 70-year-old men remarry women their own age? Is it my imagination, or are vast numbers of them now making a beeline to the younger set? I wonder if it is because they are interested in how well they can do long division. As Ricky Ricardo said best, "I don't think so Lucy!"

Men might deny this but, when push comes to shove, a shiny new model seems to attract them more. So how does this make an aging woman feel? Hating all men **could** become a national pastime for women, but why would we give them that satisfaction? Instead let's live the life **we** choose and one which will never judge us.

Even though our bodies seem to be drastically deteriorating we can still laugh. Instead of taking it personally when these **silly old fools** make their exit to bad choices, let's use our common sense. Without them in our lives, we will never have to worry again about how the plaid shirt and striped pants, that they **insist** upon wearing together, embarrass us.

We know the aging process for us all would slow down if it had to work its way through Congress, but since it does not we have to change our emotional thinking. At this stage of life, where we can predict the weather with our bones faster than the TV meteorologist, we must continue to chuckle.

I would be remiss if I did not say that all men are certainly not in that compromised category. There are some of us who have married a magnificent prince, who only can see the best in us, inside and out. They would **never** trade us for what we fear is the model with less milage. They view our aging as they do their own and know that the best years are yet to come!

~~~~~

Few Women Admit Their Age.
Few Men Act Theirs.

~~~~~

The Garment
That Wouldn't Go Away

For some of us, our clothes go back to when dinosaurs walked the earth. I have yet to meet a woman who has closets that are not packed as snugly as an overstuffed turkey on Thanksgiving. They can't seem to part with items of clothing that have not been worn since purchased on sale during the Truman administration.

This is really *not* just a "girl thing." Men also have favorite items of clothing that they just cannot purge themselves of and will continue to wear if not intercepted. They can show up in almost anything and think that it has been sanctioned by Versace. Time and time again we have to send them back to their closets with a threat of never letting them leave the house again.

We are told that when a garment has not been worn for a significant period of time we should just **give it up**. That is easier said than done for either sex. We all have favorite possessions and the fact that they are antiquated and out of style does not seem to factor into our reasoning.

The apparel choices we all make should directly relate to the decades we have been in existence. How often do we see people wearing completely inappropriate attire for their age? Not only did micro-minis go out with Elvis, but let's get real girls, the mirror is not lying to you. What fit then, when you were minus the extra 20 pounds that you now diligently carry around, does not fit now!

I remember owning a fine wool suit that required an entire week's paycheck to buy. I cherished that suit and each time I moved it went with me from house to house, state to state. That prized possession had more miles on it than a Rand McNally map.

After performing this senseless act for at least six years, one cool day I decided to wear it. I immediately realized that this valuable, venerated garment *I now* would not be caught dead in! For starters, it was too small and really, when did I ever think I looked good in that shade of mustard!

67

What no longer works for you, however, might be dynamite on someone else. Your trash could be a highly sought-after treasure for a person in need. Pick your wardrobe over with a vengeance. What you decide to part with, donate. Do the same with your husband's clothes and you will permanently prevent that lime green sports coat from ever traumatizing you again.

~~~~~

Laugh Your Way
Around The Corners
On The Bumpy Road Of Life

~~~~~

Tests We Pass, Tests We Fail

Did you ever hear the expression, "You are testing my patience?" Why as we grow older, does our ability to stay with one thought or activity vanish quicker than a running back on steroids? When I was younger my patience levels were amazingly high. I could focus on something of trivial value for hours without frustration or losing interest. Now, the first question I ask of any activity is," How long will it take?"

Is that because my common sense is telling me that time is at a premium? Our present state of existence **can** cease for **any** of us at **any time**. We must make the most of every moment and party hardy while we can. I am sure I do not have to tell you that the definition of "party hardy" changes as we age. By 70 it could mean a game of lawn bowling followed by a nap!

For that reason, beyond our required responsibilities, we should select carefully what activities will make up our day. I feel that the older we get, the more we **should be entitled to be** a bit more selfish about what we choose to do.

I have a sliding scale in my head which categorizes all activities. This scale starts at 10 and goes down to one. Any activity that rates as a ten would be something that I know I will enjoy and simply will find desirable to do. The activities that find themselves lower on that scale, I will with any luck avoid like the plague.

For instance, my husband told me the other night that the finals of the Stanley Cup were on and he asked me if I would like to join him in watching the game. My interest in hockey lasts for about 37 seconds on a good day and therefore, as an activity, would fall to the lower end of my scale. Never wanting intentionally to hurt his feelings however, I report to him that the oven needs a good cleaning and I will be *so* sorry to miss the game. He *gets that* because he of course does the same to me.

What men are interested in can fit in a pea pod. They have a narrow window which they pride themselves on keeping closed. In this same vein is their resistance to change. Any woman entering the sacrament of marriage should be fully aware of this and **never** delude yourself to think that you might be the first to succeed in changing a man.

If you try this I promise your marriage won't stay together even with Velcro. If a man even senses that you might be making this attempt, he will be more irritated than a civil rights activist. I am not saying that men will never change but the odds are about as good as Snoopy winning at Hialeah.

Men also have short fuses. They can turn red in the face and appear to be close to combustion over the least little thing. Observe them when they are interrupted during their enjoyment of the evening news. Even though they know it will be repeated every hour on the hour on a multitude of stations, they can, on the spot, turn into a spoiled seven-year-old having just had their tiny, toy truck taken away.

Again, I digress. What does all this have to do with aging? Well, we all know that what we would go to battle about in our twenties might not even get our attention in our sixties and seventies. By then most of us have learned what is **_truly important_**. We will keep our principles but know that most of what happens in our daily lives is not worth a major skirmish. A sense of humor can disarm even the most contentious situation.

~~~~~

Keep It Light To Enjoy The Night.
There Is Nothing Funny About A Fight.

~~~~~

The Driverless Car
Or, Shrink You Are It

With the onslaught of old age comes another dilemma. At some point in our lives, a decision has to be made about whether we are capable of continuing to drive. If we still feel up to the challenge, we accept the formal invitation issued by the Registry of Motor Vehicles to come in for testing. During this process they evaluate our ability to navigate a vehicle while not destroying things along our route.

Our eroding eyesight is also tested and, if we pass, a new, significantly older-looking image of ourselves is taken before we are sent on our way. This daunting process is as pleasant as dining on afterbirth but, ***once again*** we hopefully have dodged a bullet and are legal for yet another few years.

Even with license in hand, some of us should not be driving! Have you ever followed a car that looks driverless? This is a phenomenon that I find amazing. How do shrunken five foot women see over the dash of a two ton car? Well, they do! Even those of us who do not have fully operational parts still seem to manage to control this legal weapon *well* into our twilight years.

It is not surprising that we are reluctant to give up this privilege. Driving is representational of our freedom and continuing to do so is a small confirmation that we can continue to be independent. I congratulate those who stick with it even if they occasionally forget to turn off the directional signal or drive 10 miles per hour slower than a wounded wallaby. Go for it, girls! Why would anyone want to sit around and listen to their heart beat when they could be enjoying a sale at Sears?

~~~~~

Middle Age Is When You Are
Faced With Two Temptations And
You Choose The One That Will Get
You Home By Nine O'Clock.

Ronald Reagan

~~~~~

Canes, Planes And Automobiles

An amazing amount of aids are now on the market to facilitate the mobility of elders. Canes and walkers used to be the *de rigueur* of any compromised senior citizen. Today's choices of these products are varied and numerous.

Manufacturers have stepped up to the plate by designing and producing products that keep us all moving and allow us more comfort. This is a wise choice on their part since our society, as a whole, is living longer and thereby has different needs. These newly developed products are very helpful to those of us who are determined to continue to fully participate in life.

My own precious mother has just acquired a shiny new, red motorized scooter. These have been designed for any person with a depreciated ability to walk and are especially welcomed by women who have been unable to conduct their weekly pilgrimages to the mall.

It is very chic and allows transportation with great style. I have noticed in the short time that Mother has owned hers, how other ladies point and stare. She is undeniably the envy of the senior jet set!

I was a little worried at first that with her significantly arthritic hands that she would not be able to maneuver it very easily and safely. Boy, was I wrong!

On her very first attempt, off she went without trepidation. I am always happy to accompany her on her trips to the mall but since she has acquired this new mode of travel, I often find myself breathless as I am forced to run just to keep up. "Are you tired dear?" she says. "Shall I slow up for you?"

Through my heavy panting I stubbornly say, "Heck no Mom, I'm doing fine." After taking my pulse, and with one final sprint, I gratefully catch up.

At 60, am I too young to make a like investment? I can clearly envision us riding in tandem, passing and waving to all those unfortunate people who have not moved into this century of shopping.

This Is The Bottom Line, So Pay Attention

We rush through life for what? To what? To get to the end sooner? No sir. Not me. I want to stick around for a long time. So I intend to slow it up and take in more of the view. I will accept those varicose veins that are now the road map of my life.

Everyone goes through bad times and when you have had a terrible event happen in your life you are entitled to some serious TLC. Life is difficult, especially when problems are painfully limiting or disabling. That's where husbands, life partners, family members and close friends come in handy. Look to them for advice and even sympathy.

DON'T FORGET, YOUR THOUGHTS ARE YOUR REALITY.

But remember, the more you believe things are bad the longer they will be bad. You will never be able to appreciate *any* good in your life if you are bogged down with a continuous stream of negative thoughts. The more time you spend in that place of despondency, the harder it will be for you to crawl back out into the sun. Encourage yourself to find *whatever* there is that is positive and happy and make it your focus.

Life is imperfect and so are we. So the best advice to us all is to accept our imperfect bodies. Be grateful for what they do for us *successfully* each day and forgive them for what they do not do. Being on this planet is not always easy but it is worth it.

DO NOT ALLOW YOURSELF TO LIVE IN THE LAND OF REGRET!

So after a reasonable period, put on your big-girl panties and get over it. Today is a new day. Work with what God has given you and make the best of it. Mark Twain once said" I did not attend her funeral but I did send a letter saying I approved of it." Let's not be *that* person!

Life is like a roll of toilet paper. The closer it gets to the end the faster it goes. So don't waste even a day.

TAKE A MOMENT TO BE IN EACH MOMENT.

Be glad God didn't give us everything we asked for. After all there is a divine plan for each of us and woe be it for us to question *that*. Life is for learning lessons and one important lesson is not to take yourself too seriously.

FINDING THE HUMOR, FINDS THE JOY.

Appreciate the scenery along the way, even when you are forced to take a detour. If what you have today is gone tomorrow, you always have those twenty-year-old bathing suit pictures to look back on.

Have no fear, my dear. When you age, you turn the page. Just make sure you continue to enjoy each chapter of *your* book. "I've had a perfectly wonderful life but this wasn't it," *should not* be your mantra.

It's all about attitude. The past is old news and the future is a wonderful adventure waiting to happen. Take the fast train out of desperation and allow that visit to the mirror to be enjoyable.

Learn how to be fully alive and *don't forget to smile*. A friendly, warm smile will direct the viewer away from cheesecake hips any day! At whatever age you are, strut your stuff. You are the best. Believe it because you are the woman *beyond the mirror!*

CPSIA information can be obtained at www.ICGtesting.com
Printed in the USA
BVOW040527220812

298295BV00004B/4/P

9 781938 135521